MY NEW SOCIAL LIFE

DOMINIQUE DORVIL

Outskirts Press, Inc.
Denver, Colorado

Outskirts Press, Inc.
http://www.outskirtspress.com

ISBN: 978-1-4327-7012-9

Outskirts Press and the "OP" logo are trademarks belonging to Outskirts Press, Inc.

PRINTED IN THE UNITED STATES OF AMERICA

For Mom and Dad

ACKNOWLEDGMENTS

I am grateful that God gave me the talent to write books. I also thank Manfred Dorvil, Mildred Prosper, Cassandre Dorvil, and Elise Connors.

CHAPTER ONE

I was sitting with the popular girls at lunchtime. I didn't like hanging out with them, but I didn't think I had a choice since I didn't have any real friends. School started a month ago and I still had no friends that I *enjoyed* being around! Everyone else had friends except me.

"Look at Lyric. Her hair doesn't even look right on her," Tessa Burton remarked.

The girl Tessa was talking about was Lyric Ramos. She had her hair in a bob. She was really talkative. I didn't like her much but I didn't talk bad about her either, like Tessa or Savannah Hyde, one of Tessa's "best friends."

I once heard this girl in my class say that the popular girls just think that they are popular, which I don't understand because how do you *think* you are popular? My mom thinks that you have to know it. Well, they are just both opinions. And opinions aren't facts; they are what you think. So maybe both of them are wrong.

"I know. Where did she get it anyway?" Savannah asked.

"What's so wrong about her hairstyle?" I asked. They all turned their attention to me. "What?" I asked, even though I knew exactly why they were staring at me like that.

"Do you like it?" Savannah asked in disgust.

"Who cares?" Tessa said. "Have you seen the way Bertha has

been acting? She is so weird." The girl they were talking about was Bertha Vela. She was their best friend. She was the least mean out of all of them.

Savannah rolled her eyes. "Yeah. Bertha isn't even cool. She always acts like she's cool but she's not."

"She's just sick. If you were sick—wait a minute, that's not even weird. That's normal," I replied. "Just because she had a runny nose doesn't mean she's weird." They all looked at me again.

Candace Chavez, Tessa's other friend, came over and sat in the empty seat next to me.

"Do you know Bradley?" Candace asked.

"Who?" I asked.

They all looked at me. *Again.*

"What?"

Tessa held her hand in front of my face and said, "You don't know *Bradley Goodyear?*"

"Yeah. He's like a two- timer. He dated—" Savannah said.

"How do you know all about that?" Candace interrupted.

"I heard the eighth graders talking about it," Savannah said.

"Listen," Candace scolded. "I'm telling this story and I'm the *only* one who's going to be talking…" Candace looked at Tessa.

"Until I say so," Tessa approved.

"What about Bradley?" I asked. Now I was getting into it. All I wanted to know was who Bradley Goodyear was and why Candace was talking about him.

"Yeah," Tessa said. "What about him?"

"He asked me out," Candace answered.

"No, he didn't," Tessa said as she high-fived Candace. "Are you going to say yes?"

Candace rolled her eyes. "I don't know."

I swallowed the last piece of my brownie and said, "Why would you want to go out with a person who's a two-timer?"

"Yeah," Savannah replied. Savannah usually always disagrees with what I say.

While they were arguing about if Candace should date Bradley, I was looking at everyone else. The other kids were laughing and hanging out with fun people. I was sort of jealous but not in a way that Tessa and her—I mean *my*—"friends" acted. Like when Bertha said her mom bought the iPod Touch and Tessa and Bertha didn't talk for two weeks. Bertha was sitting by herself.

I didn't really want to sit with Tessa. Tessa could be mean sometimes. And sometimes she could be a real friend. Not that she was officially my friend or whatever. Anyway, Lyric was talking like usual to her friends, who hardly seemed to mind all her talking. Sometimes I wondered what they talked about. I wished I had some real friends. Maybe something good would happen today.

"So do you think she should?" Savannah asked me.

"She should do what?" I questioned.

She rolled her eyes. "Weren't you listening? I'm talking about Candace."

I didn't say anything. I didn't really care about what Savannah had to say.

"I don't care, okay?" I answered her with an attitude.

"Don't talk to me like that!" Savannah screamed in my face.

"If you talk to me that way, then I can," I remarked. I was very proud of myself. I mean, before I would have never have done what I just did: stand up for myself. Tessa started whispering to Savannah.

"Yeah. He really is cute," Savannah said.

I rolled my eyes. Whatever. This was the kind of stuff I was sick and tired of. This was what I was dealing with.

CHAPTER TWO

I turned around in my chair in social studies. My teacher, Ms. Class, had left the room, and this boy I had a crush on named Jaxon Lovejoy was staring right at me.

"Hi, Jaxon," I said.

"Hey, Brylee. Um, what's up?" Jaxon said.

"Well, actually—" I replied.

"Hi, baby," Tessa said, then glared at me.

"Excuse?" he asked.

"C'mon, baby. Aren't we boyfriend and girlfriend?" Tessa remarked.

"Since when?" Jaxon replied.

I couldn't believe Tessa would do this. Not that I had told her he was my crush, but it was still not fair. Jaxon *was* the cutest boy in the class, so who wouldn't have a crush on him? But still it was *my* special moment with *him*.

"Since last week when you came to my house and we were *kissing*," Tessa replied.

Jaxon leaned and looked at me, then said, "We were never kissing. Brylee, you believe me, right?"

"Maybe she would believe me if I did this," Tessa replied. She kissed Jaxon on the *lips*. I couldn't believe this. This was ludicrous and a disgrace!

Jaxon frowned. "What's your problem, you…"

Tessa waited. He didn't say anything so she moved on.

"You don't have to be shy to tell her. Besides, you know you liked it when we kissed."

"We never kissed!" he screamed.

"He never kissed you!" I said. Just then Ms. Class came in right at that moment I screamed at Tessa.

"Excuse me. Jaxon, Tessa, and Brylee, come with me. *Now!*" Ms. Class yelled.

"But what did we do?" Jaxon questioned. Jaxon was so cute when he was frustrated.

Tessa just laughed at him. "Oh, baby. You are so cute when you're frustrated."

I couldn't believe she said that! It was almost as if she was just sabotaging my moment with him on purpose.

"Stop calling me that!" he yelled.

"Leave this room now!" my teacher screamed even louder. When Ms. Class screams it's really loud; it's almost like when Tessa yelled because Bertha stepped on her manicured finger by accident.

"Why do you hang out with her anyway?" Jaxon whispered.

"I have no friends so I don't really have a choice," I replied.

"Of course you have a choice. Tessa is just trying to make you jealous and you know it." He smiled at me. "Because you like me?"

"Yeah. I do. I really do." I know that was a stupid thing to say, but I couldn't lie to him.

"Well, I—" he started.

"Why were you kissing him, girls?" Ms. Class asked when we stepped into the hallway.

"I didn't kiss him," I protested.

"Yes," Tessa said. "I saw you. You kissed him and you know it."

"If you both didn't, then who did?" my teacher questioned.

"I did not. I even have proof," Tessa said. She went into the room and started talking to Savannah. Savannah walked up to us.

"Do you know which one of them kissed him?" Ms. Class asked.

"Yes, I do, Ms. Class. Brylee was kissing him," Savannah lied. "Then she started bragging that it felt *nice* and then she started screaming at Tessa. She said she and Jaxon are boyfriend and girlfriend."

"*Excuse me.* Did I just hear what I thought I heard?" my teacher said. "Why would you let her *kiss* you, Jaxon? Do you like her? Tell me the truth."

"Yes," Jaxon answered.

I can't believe he just said that. I mean, he likes me!

"I'm giving you two a note home. How dare you kiss in my classroom!" Ms. Class looked at Tessa and Savannah. "You know what. I'm going to—"

"No!" a voice cried.

"Lyric?" Ms. Class said in a stern voice.

"Jaxon and Brylee didn't kiss," Lyric replied.

"Lyric, you talked too late. They are getting in trouble and that's final," Ms. Class remarked. "Go to your seats."

We did as we were told. Tessa was whispering to her friends and then they started pointing and laughing at me; however, Ms. Class didn't scream at them. All she did was glare at them. I was so mad. I mean, Tessa was laughing at me. I couldn't believe this. Wait. I actually could believe what she did. You could tell Jaxon felt the same way because he wasn't talking to me the way he usually did.

I guess Tessa wasn't my "friend" anymore. Now I absolutely had nothing *like* friends, with the exception of Jaxon. It was actually better when she was being mean than having no friends at all.

CHAPTER THREE

"Why did you do that for me?" I asked Lyric as we were walking home. Lyric was my neighbor, but I never talked to her before today.

"Well…" she began. "I wanted to help you because I know you didn't kiss Jaxon. Plus, I saw Tessa kiss him."

"Really?" I questioned.

"Yeah. But it would have been nice if you *did* kiss him."

"Why?" I asked, even though I knew the answer.

"Because he's cute. You are really lucky. You sit right behind him!"

"And?"

"A lot of girls would want your seat."

"But isn't sitting next to him better?"

"No, silly. There are boys surrounding him, so you are the only girl around him."

"True." We were really quiet for a while. We were almost near our houses. I was so bored I decided to observe which house had more foliage. Nevertheless it was boring. Thank goodness Lyric broke the silence.

"I know Tessa and her friends were talking about me today."

"Yeah," I replied.

"And you tried to defend me."

"How did you know?"

"I was listening." She looked at the ground. "I also observe," she added.

"What are you talking about?"

She hesitated. "I see the way you act around Tessa, Savannah, and the other ones."

"So?"

"Why do you hang out with them, anyway?"

"I have no one to hang out with."

"You can hang out with us." She stopped walking. "Don't you ever wonder if they talk about you behind your back?"

"No."

"Well, they do. Just to let you know."

"How do you know?"

"I heard Savannah and Candace talking about you in the bathroom."

I ran away. I went into the park. No one was at the park so I sat on the swing and wept. Usually the swings were full. I cried for probably four minutes until Lyric spotted me.

"You don't have to cry," Lyric assured me as she sat down next to me.

"Well, I thought that they were my friends."

"They will never be your friends," she corrected me.

"But I thought they were. They fooled me!"

"Calm down. You can come to my house. I know the perfect thing to make you happy."

"What?" I asked.

"Can't tell. It's a surprise."

"So do you think your friends will accept me?"

"Yes!"

We walked quickly to her house. I was really happy because I finally found someone to make me happy. I just hoped her friends accepted me. I mean, they had never talked to me before, so I didn't know what they were like. However, I did know what Lyric was like: she was talkative and argumentative.

CHAPTER FOUR

"Hello, honey… oh, you have a friend," Lyric's mom said when we walked through the doorway. She didn't look happy when she saw me.

"Hi, my name is Brylee," I introduced myself.

"Hi, um, Lyric, what did I tell you about inviting people over without permission?"

"She's just a friend!" Lyric replied. She crossed her arms and rolled her eyes.

"You could bring in a murderer or a stalker in here for all I know!"

"Shut up," Lyric muttered.

Lyric's mom held up her finger at her daughter and said, "Watch your—"

"Maybe I should just leave," I suggested, but they weren't even listening because they were bickering. I walked out the door and went home. I hoped Lyric wouldn't think it was rude of me to leave without saying good-bye. But if she did think it was rude, it wouldn't matter because her mother was rude to me.

"Hi, Mom," I said as I opened my front door.

"Hi, honey. How was your day at school today? And use a word that your little cousin doesn't know." My mom wanted me to use other types of words instead of *fun, exciting, boring, more boring*, etc. She wanted me to use words like *productive*.

"My day was rowdy."

"How?"

"Because Tessa kissed this boy I like in my class. And then I got in trouble."

"How did you—"

"I don't want to talk about it, okay?" I interrupted.

"Do you want to help me with dinner?" she asked as she stirred some orange stuff in a pot.

"No, I'm okay."

I went upstairs. I sat in my bedroom and stared at the wall. I didn't know what to do and I didn't have any homework. Suddenly, it got really quiet in my room.

I took a glimpse into my sister's room. She was sound asleep. I crept into her room to see if she was faking but she wasn't. I decided to use this opportunity to put whip cream in her hand. I sauntered down the stairs and into the kitchen where my mom was reading a book.

"Hi, honey. I didn't call dinner," my mom said.

"Oh, I know. I need some whip cream."

"It's finished."

I stood there for a moment and decided to use ketchup. It was better that I use ketchup rather than whip cream because my sister Brynn hated ketchup. I took it and ran up the steps. I squeezed the ketchup bottle in her hand, once I got in the room. I took a feather that she used as a bookmark and I put it over her nose, and then ran out without making a sound.

"AH!!!!!" a voice screamed and I started laughing. "MOM! I was bleeding in my sleep!"

I heard my mom coming up the steps and she said, "There must be some— AH!!!! You have *blood* on your face."

She ran out of Brynn's room.

"Hey, this isn't blood. This is—"

I laughed so hard until my stomach ached.

"*You* did this!" she screamed at me.

"No, I didn't. That was Rylee." Rylee was my other sister. "She's doing homework."

"Yeah. But you know that she's sneaky and that she's foolish. Why would I do that to my favorite sister?" I lied. Neither of them was really my favorite. It usually changed because usually they did something to get me pissed off.

"You're right. She is foolish."

"Why were you sleeping, anyway?"

"Remember Ms. Wilis?" I nodded. "Yeah. She has been giving a lot of work. And the work we don't finish in class is our homework. She doesn't even give everyone the same work. She says she does that because she doesn't want anyone to cheat. My friend Azura is mad at Grady, her boyfriend, and talked to me nonstop."

"Yeah, whatever," I replied, turning out the door. "Wait." I turned back around. "Why is she pissed at her boyfriend?"

My sister smiled. "She thinks she's cheating on her with my other friend Pauline."

"Did Pauline ever come here?"

"Yeah. We had to do this science project and—" she informed.

"I don't care," I interrupted.

CHAPTER FIVE

My mom drove me to school. It was really quiet. "I'm still not happy about what you did yesterday. You scared me." My mom broke the silence. I didn't say anything. "*Ketchup?* Really? Then you blame it on Rylee?"

"Well, I was just bored. And Rylee is silly," I replied.

"Hey. I heard that you know," Rylee said.

"It's true, Rylee," Brynn replied.

"Prove it," Rylee demanded.

"When you had a sleepover, you wrote on your friend's forehead 'Crazy,'" I replied.

"Whatever. That's all you can think of? Wow. You have a bad memory." She looked out the window. "Just to let you know, that is not silly."

Mom pulled up in front of the school building even though I begged on my knees for her not to do that. All she said was:

"I'm the driver, dear. When you have to drop me somewhere I won't tell you, 'Don't stop right in front of the building.'"

"Well, I guess I'm sticking with you guys," Brynn said.

"Why? Don't you hang out with your other stupid friends?" Rylee ked hanging out with us at school. She thought s" her in front of her friends.

much and they are giving me headaches with ," our sister answered.

"And this is our problem because?" Rylee asked.

"Why can't she just hang out with us?" I asked.

"What a stupid question. I have friends that I have to meet. Okay?" She said it like I was younger than she was, which I was, but there was only a two-year difference.

"You can hang out with me," I replied. I actually wanted her to come with me just in case Lyric's friends didn't like me.

"Thank you," Rylee remarked, then sauntered into the school-yard without saying good-bye. How rude. However, if you lived with Rylee for your whole life, you would expect that.

I looked around until I found Lyric. She was talking to her friends and her friends looked really angry. Two of them look identical. Brynn and I walked over and this is what I heard:

"...we can't accept Brylee—" Lyric said. This was devastating. Dreadful. How could they do this? How could *she* do this to *me*?

"She's right behind you," Sunshine Donovan said.

"Yeah. *She's* behind you," I replied. I was so outraged. "You... I can't believe you. You said..."

"No! I didn't say anything bad. They are the ones who don't like you," Lyric said.

"Why are you even trying to lie to me?"

"How dare you lie to my sister! What kind of person are you?" my sister remarked. "Are you lying?"

Brynn walked up to Lyric's face. So close that it looked like they were going to kiss.

"No. I'm not lying," she replied.

Her friends walked away.

"Hey, don't walk away!" Lyric yelled to her friends.

Brynn walked toward them. "If any of you know if Lyric is lying, you better tell me. I'm an eighth grader and I can beat you up every day," she lied. I should thank her for all this progress.

They started to look scared, although none of them said anything.

"I'll start beating you guys up tomorrow."

"Why tomorrow?" Charlie Snider asked.

"So you can think about it."

The other girls scattered away.

"I'm not lying, Brylee," Lyric said.

I looked at her in disgust. "Yeah, right." I walked off and brushed my shoulders off with hers. I was fuming. I couldn't believe that she was still lying to me.

"Brylee!" a voice called.

"What?" I turned around and it was my sister.

I watched her walk toward me. "Are you okay? I mean, you looked really angry."

"No. I can't believe she would lie to me."

"I don't think she was lying."

I rolled my eyes. "*Whose* side are you on?"

"Whose side are *you* on?" she said, then walked away.

I couldn't believe this. Now who was I going to talk to? Two thoughts passed my mind: number one, start talking to myself. Number two: buy a diary and write in it. I decided to do them both.

"Hey there," I whispered. "I really... Okay, this is totally not working out."

I decided to work on number two. Actually I really didn't like either of those ideas.

CHAPTER SIX

The next day, it was raining, so we had to sit in the auditorium. I wasn't talking to anyone, so I started to eavesdrop on what people were saying:

"We have so much homework."

"I think she likes Mr. Feldman. She always laughs when he's around."

"I wasn't even lying to Brylee. She only heard the part when I was repeating what Sunshine and the others were saying." I turned around and it was Lyric.

"I believe you now," I confided.

Her face brightened. "Really?"

I nodded. "Yeah. I do."

"They don't like you."

"Why?" I shook my head. "What did I do to them?"

"It's because you hang out with Tessa, Savannah, Bertha, and whoever else."

"Bertha's not that mean. And I'm not mean. Why can't they just give me a chance?"

"Maybe you should stop hanging out with them and then they'll accept you, I guess."

"Like…hang out with my sister?"

"Your sister is scary. I thought she was going to hurt me for real."

"She really would have if she wanted to yesterday."

"Is she popular or something?"

"Yeah. You can say that," I fibbed so I wouldn't have to blow up her spot.

"So. Just hang out with your sister... Actually don't."

"Why?" I questioned.

"Because they don't like her either," she replied.

"GET TO CLASS!" Ms. Pattison yelled into the microphone. "NOW! NOW, NOW, NOW!"

"She doesn't have to scream *that* loud," Lyric said.

"Who were you talking to?" I asked.

"Oh. This girl from my cooking class."

"Oh," I replied. Then I spotted Sunshine. She was hiding her face but I noticed her green bag. "Look. There's Sunshine."

"Really?" She walked over to her. They talked and Sunshine's face brightened. Then Lyric pointed at me. She walked back over.

"Sunshine said she'll *try* to give you a chance," Lyric informed me.

I smiled widely. I was on the road to friendship!

CHAPTER SEVEN

In social studies, Ms. Class kept staring at me. Then, she started taking notes.

Sunshine raised her hand. "Why do you keep looking in that direction?" Sunshine pointed at me and Jaxon.

"Don't you remember what happened?" Lyric asked.

"Brylee was making out with Jaxon," Tessa called out.

"No, I wasn't!" I yelled.

"Jaxon and Brylee sitting in the tree. K-I-S-S..." a group of kids sang.

"Shut it!" Ms. Class screamed.

Jaxon passed me a note. It said:

I can't believe that was happening! You weren't even making out with me. Even though I would have liked to, I didn't.

P.S.

Do you like me? Yes or no?

"Why are you passing notes?" Ms. Class questioned. "Give it to me." I gave her the note. To my horror, she read the note out loud.

A group of kids started saying, "Oooo. Jaxon likes..."

I started to blush. I could feel it. I stayed really quiet. I didn't even raise my hand for anything. Not even to use the bathroom. And the thing was that I didn't even get to answer his question. But why would he ask me that question twice?

Finally, the class was over. It was finally lunchtime.

"When's the wedding?" Megan Puckett asked.

"What wedding?" I asked.

"You and Jaxon."

"There is no wedding."

She ignored that. "Can I be the flower girl?" I looked at her and walked away.

"Where's your boyfriend?" Nelson Barlow, Jaxon's friend, asked.

"Jaxon is not my boyfriend," I answered.

"You better stay close to your man. He's a *real* chick magnet," Reese Hahn said in between laughs.

I sighed. "Whatever." I sat down next to Lyric. There was an empty seat next to me. As soon as I looked at it, the seat was taken in a blink of an eye.

It wasn't Sunshine. It was Brynn.

As she sat down she said, "Hello."

I waved.

She glared at Sunshine the way she did when there was only one last piece of chicken at the dinner table. "I said I was going to beat you up today. Are you ready?"

"No. I decided to give her a chance," Sunshine replied.

"That wasn't the question!" my sister yelled.

"Calm down. Lyric wasn't lying," I whispered.

Brynn reached in her lunch bag for an apple and said, "She better not be."

"Better not be what?" I quizzed.

"She better not be lying. Duh!"

Sunshine was staring at us.

"I think you're scaring her."

"Scaring whom?"

I sighed. "Forget it."

CHAPTER EIGHT

"Why do we have to eat lunch outside?" Sunshine questioned.

"Because there was a flood in the basement," I replied.

"How was there a flood in the basement?" Lyric asked.

"Because it was raining last night. You never knew that?" Brynn replied.

Sunshine leaned over to Lyric and said something. Then Lyric leaned over to me and whispered, "Sunshine said that your sister is getting on her nerves."

"What do you want me to do about that?" I replied.

"To make her leave."

"I can't make her leave. She has nowhere to go," I answered.

"I'll get her a friend."

"How?"

"My cousin goes to this school. And he can hang out with your sister," Lyric stated.

I frowned. "How am I going to do that? Say, 'Oh, get out of my table'?"

"Let me say it then." She tapped my sister on the shoulder before she got to put her ham sandwich in her mouth. She looked at Lyric. "Um, I think it's better for you to hang out with your own peers."

"You are my peers," my sister stated.

"Well… I mean, people exactly your age."

"Oh." She smirked. However, she frowned again. "My friends—"

"Forget your friends. I know this boy named Cody and he's my cousin. You can hang out with him," Lyric interrupted.

"Or," I chimed in, "you can start talking to your friends again."

"Or you can agree with my plan."

It took Brynn some time to make her decision.

"I'll go with my sister's plan," Brynn decided.

"You can go now," Sunshine murmured.

Brynn glared at her. "Maybe I should stay."

"NO!" we roared.

"Okay. I'll leave."

"Thank you," Sunshine said.

"So where's the rest of you?" I asked.

"Oh. We're having a contest," Sunshine replied.

"A contest on what?" I questioned.

Sunshine took a sip of her juice. "We're trying to see how long we can stay away from each other."

I rolled my eyes. "Yeah."

CHAPTER NINE

"Don't you think the contest you guys are doing is boring?" I asked.

Sunshine's eyes widened. *"Boring?"* she said with her mouth full of tuna. "How is this contest boring?" She made air quotes on "boring."

"Well…" Lyric said. "It is—"

"THE ONLY REASON YOU THINK IT'S BORING IS BECAUSE YOU DIDN'T THINK OF IT YOURSELF!" Then she stomped away.

"She's got some issues," Lyric said.

"Then why are you friends with her?"

She rolled her eyes. "I don't know. It's complicated." She chewed her apple, swallowed it, and finished, "We— I mean my friends and I don't like her."

"Then just stop talking to her."

She giggled like I had said the most humorous thing in the world. "You're joking, right?"

"Tell me all the bad things about her."

"Well, she gets her attitude at us for no reason. She's harsh, hard-hearted, stubborn, and a bully," Lyric said.

"That," I answered, "is it?"

She nodded. "I can't name them from the top of my head."

We stayed quiet for a long time. I was staring at Jaxon. He was so cute. Plus, he ran so fast. Reese caught the ball and threw it at someone I didn't recognize.

"So...are you usually this boring?" I asked.

"No. I just don't know you so..."

"Then try to get to know me."

She turned away from the boys playing football. "Okay. Do you like Jaxon?"

"Jaxon? Why are you asking about him?" I asked as I tried not to make myself laugh.

"You're a total giveaway."

"What? I'm not laughing."

"But you're smiling." She smiled at me. Her was smile so wide that I could see her missing tooth. "Tell me the truth. You know you like him."

"So..."

"You guys passed notes. You read what it said on the note. He likes you."

"Whatever," I said.

"What's your favorite color?"

"Green, orange, and blue."

She pursed her lips. "See? I knew you liked him." Her eyes expanded. "He's right behind you."

"Hi, Brylee," Jaxon greeted me. "What are you up to?"

"Nothing." I glanced at Lyric. She was smiling. I rolled my eyes at her foolishness.

"So what's your answer?" Jaxon asked.

"What answer?"

"The note I passed to you." I was confused. I had absolutely no idea what he was talking about. He leaned closer to me. So close I could smell what he had for lunch. "I like you," he whispered.

We stared at each other. "I—"

The bell rang.

"We've got to go," Lyric said as she grabbed my wrist.

"Bye," I said to Jaxon. He waved back at me.

"Oh my gosh! He likes you. What did he whisper in your ear?"

"Loser," Sunshine said as she hit Lyric's head.

What was *that* all about?

CHAPTER TEN

I was so delighted about my day that I was beaming. I almost felt like a different person. I even smiled at Ms. Class when I saw her in the hallway. And I knew middle school would be a blast.

"You know what I heard?" Lyric said with a sly look on her face.

"What?" I asked enthusiastically.

Lyric jumped up and down before telling me. "Jaxon is going to ask you out!"

"Really?"

"Nope!" She covered her mouth to cover her grin; nevertheless, I could hear her hooting away.

I frowned. "That's not funny. You know I like him."

"Oh. So now you want to admit it," she said as she laughed. "Your mom won't even let you go out with boys."

"How do you know?" I asked.

"Because my mom doesn't want me to go out with boys. What's the big deal? You're not even going anywhere!"

"Yeah. I wonder why they call it that when you're not even going anywhere."

"But I basically just said that."

"So."

"Hey, Brylee," Megan said.

"Hi, Megan," I replied. Megan walked away. Megan never really talked to me. At first no one really talked to me except Jaxon. That was one of the reasons I liked him. However, now people were talking to me.

"Since when does Megan start talking to you?"

I shrugged. "I don't know."

"I can't believe we have a bunch of tests next week. Like our French test..."

"Math tests. Are they trying to kill us?"

"No. They are just making sure we know what we're supposed to know."

"All at the same time?"

"True. Well, at least I'm good at testing."

"Really?" I asked.

"Yes," Lyric testified.

"What score did you get on your social studies test last week?"

"A fifty-five." I gave her a look. "That's only because I was at Red Lobster for my mother's birthday."

"C'mon. Let's go," I said, rushed.

"Why are you in such a hurry?" Lyric asked.

"I just want to finish my homework and get some sleep for the next day."

"How will you finish your homework? We have so much. Mrs. Frost gave us four writing assignments."

"So?" I replied.

"They are boring!"

"And?"

"That means it will take a long time to do."

"Okay then. All you have to do is think about it while you're doing your other homeworks."

"'Homeworks?'"

"What?"

"I don't think that's the right word."

"I don't care." We staggered out of the lobby and outside. It was crowded as usual. Nevertheless, it was probably just nothing.

"FIGHT! FIGHT! FIGHT! FIGHT!" hollered the crowd.

"Who's fighting?" Lyric said.

A girl in front of us turned around. It was Megan. "Jaxon and Reese are fighting. Jaxon knows how to fight!" She peeked at me. "Now you know you'll be protected." She giggled at her own joke.

"Can *we* see what's going on?" I asked.

"Sure," Megan replied.

What I saw was…was…horrible. Reese had a scratch and the worst thing about it was that blood was coming out of it.

"Isn't that gross?" asked Lyric.

I couldn't believe Jaxon did that. I really couldn't believe he would do that.

"Where's the principal?" a girl in the front row asked.

Jaxon tried to punch Reese, but he missed. Then Reese ducked and ran past me. I felt a drip of water on me.

"Well, I can't believe I don't have my umbrella," Megan whined.

"That's weird. You're the most organized person I know," I replied. "But not more organized than my mom. Her closet is organized alphabetically."

"Can I come with you guys?" Megan questioned.

CHAPTER ELEVEN

"That was an awesome fight. You should have been there from the beginning," Megan said. She'd been talking for the last twenty minutes. "People say I talk a lot. Is that true?"

"No," Lyric and I said in unison.

Megan wiped her forehead. "Thank goodness. Do you feel sorry for Reese?"

"Why?" I asked.

"Why," Lyric said, "do you talk about one thing and after that you talk about something else; then you talk about the first thing you talked about?"

"What do you mean?" Megan replied.

"Never mind. Continue what you were saying," I stated.

"I said that because Reese fell and looked like he was wounded really badly," Megan informed me.

"Why did the fight begin anyway?" Lyric asked.

"Because someone said that Reese was talking about Jaxon. Jaxon was furious."

"Jaxon made the first move, right?" I quizzed.

"Of course." Megan stopped to tie her sneakers.

"I didn't know he could fight," I said.

Megan got up and said, "He was always like that. In second grade he choked me."

"Why?" Lyric asked.

"Who knows?" Megan retorted.

"Did he get in trouble?" I asked.

"Nope. I didn't tell. I was too scared."

I didn't know Jaxon would be like this. He choked someone? He made someone bleed? I always thought that he was sweet like candy. And not sour like a pickle.

Lyric kept looking at me, giving me smirks. In return, I just frowned. There was nothing good about that conversation.

"He was about to punch the teacher but *Reese* pulled him back," Megan continued.

"Wow," Lyric commented.

"Although, there was this day a kid punched him in his face. He was way bigger than Jaxon. Jaxon didn't dare do anything to *that* guy."

"Is he in this school?" Lyric questioned.

"Yeah. But he's in the Phoenix Academy and we're in the Eagle Academy. He was cute."

"He isn't cute anymore?" I replied.

"I don't know. Yes?" Megan responded.

"Can I stay at your house for a little while?" Megan asked.

"Sure," I replied. Lyric looked at me, her eyes huge.

"Do you want to hear something that's disturbing?" Megan asked.

"Here's my house," I announced.

"Wow," Megan replied as if she had never seen a house before. "Your house is nice." She stepped inside my house the moment I opened the door. "Perfectly tiled floor."

Brynn stepped in front of her. "Hello? Why are you sniffing our floor?" She remarked rudely.

"This is the best tiled floor I've *ever* seen." Megan hugged my sister. "And you smell like Victoria Secret...um..."

"Endless Love," Brynn said.

"Yes. That is my absolute favorite!" Megan glanced at my sister from the corner of her eye. "Can I use some?"

Lyric's mouth was opened slightly ajar.

"Close your mouth," I told her.

"Leave me alone," Brynn said. "I only came down here to get some apples." She walked away flipping her dark brown hair, which she always does when there are people or a cute boy around.

That really got on my nerves because when I was in the fifth grade, I wasn't interested in boys, and I had a science project to do. This cute boy was my partner, and Brynn walked ahead of us and started flipping her hair and asking me to take her picture. I mean she could at least flirt with someone her own age. Then the boy said he never wanted to see me again. To make it worse I had to do the project on my own. On the bright side I got a four plus.

"What was that all about?" Lyric asked.

"What? That perfume smells wonderful and stuff," Megan replied. I always thought Megan was like in the middle of being popular and lame...nevertheless, now she was really annoying. She did weird, crazy stuff, and she was full of surprises.

"She is full of surprises," Lyric whispered to me as if she read my mind.

"I know," I whispered back. Megan started going up the staircase and we followed her.

"Look over there," Megan instructed, and we did. Unfortunately, when we turned around she was gone. On the bright side at least she was gone. OMG! SHE WAS GONE!

"She's gone!" Lyric and I both yelled.

"AH!" a voice that sounded similar to my sister's own yelled. However, not quite.

Lyric looked around. "Maybe I should leave..."

"No, you have to stay," I said, looking the other direction as I watched my sister running out of the bathroom in her robe and shower cap.

"And you said I shouldn't leave?" my friend screamed over all the screaming. I could see a smile forming on her face.

"It's not funny." We looked at each other and then we both started to laugh.

"What's so funny?" Megan questioned.

"Nothing," I said.

"You ran through her sister's shower," Lyric confided.

"I didn't know she was in there."

"Which bathroom was she using?"

Megan looked up to the sky as if her answer was up there. "In a room that had pictures of singers, ponies, writing pieces, and paintings."

"That's her room."

"I thought it was yours. Besides, one of those writing pieces said, 'Love Brylee.'"

"I gave that to her when I was five."

Brynn came back out in purple pants and a pink shirt that had a cat on it. She was full of rage. I could tell because whenever she was angry she looked really happy.

"GET OUT OF THIS *HOUSE!*" she shrieked. Megan ran away.

"Why'd you do that for?" I quizzed. "Be nice to your guests."

"She needs to learn how to knock. The door was closed. It's a good thing that I was coming *out* of the shower."

"You know, Mom would have told you could have handled it in a better way."

"Yeah, you're right. I should have."

"Let's go start that homework," Lyric said.

CHAPTER TWELVE

The next day was weird. Sunshine kept gazing at us. The weirdest thing was that she was sitting at the table with Tessa. I overheard some stuff.

"I don't like them either," Tessa revealed. I couldn't help but notice a colorful bracelet on Tessa's arm. It looked pretty.

"They are so lame," Savannah added as she looked over at me, signaling that she was talking about me. "She used to hang out with us." She didn't exactly signal it like actually tell me. When someone is talking about you they always look at you while they are talking.

"Why did you hang out with *that* loser?" Sunshine questioned. Now that was offensive. To me at least. One of my old friends in fifth grade called my other friend a loser and she just shrugged her shoulders.

"Loser" is offensive to me because it just sounds mean. Even when you are playing a game and you lose and someone says the winner of this tournament is…whoever it is…and the loser of this tournament is…whoever, it just sounds plain mean. People could say "the person who lost," "the person who didn't have that much luck," or "the person who didn't get the victory."

"We should start to call them losers," Candace suggested with a smirk.

Yes, I told her this in the beginning of the year when I thought we were friends. I felt angry. However, I just forgave them because karma would get them.

The bell rang and it was time to go to gym. I told Lyric everything I heard. This is what she said:

"You don't know if they were talking about you." I just laughed and shook my head.

I headed toward the girls' locker room and I saw Charlie. Charlie saw me too. She was with another girl, Anna Torres.

"Hi, Brylee," Charlie greeted. I waved.

"Where were you at lunch?" Lyric asked Charlie.

"I was in the main office getting my bus pass" answered Charlie. "Hi, Anna," Lyric answered.

"Hi, Brylee and Lyric."

"Hi," I asked. But I couldn't help but notice that Anna had the same colorful bracelet that Tessa had. Several thoughts popped into my head: *Did she steal it? Did she borrow it? Do they just have the same thing? Was she the culprit of that missing gym shirt last month?*

"Nice bracelet," I commented.

"Thank you. I just got it today. *Someone* gave it to me," Anna informed me.

I gulped. She stole it! I quickly walked into the locker room. Tessa was in there blabbing about some movie she saw with her boyfriend last night. First of all, she was too young to be having a boyfriend. Well, at least that was what my mom said. Second, yesterday she said she was going to a party at her cousin's house. Aha! It's not the same. I mean, boyfriends and cousins aren't the same people.

"Hey, can I try on your bracelet?" Savannah asked. I looked at the bracelet and gulped. She had it. It was okay and there was no way Anna could have stolen it.

"Mind your business," Sunshine said.

I guess I gulped too loud and was staring at them too long. I turned around and saw Anna.

I walked around her and left. In gym, there was another class that came in with us. It was the seventh grade chorus. As I left the locker room I saw one of the seventh grade girls leave with a bracelet that looked just like Tessa's. Maybe I was going crazy or something but I knew I wasn't.

CHAPTER THIRTEEN

Tessa was meaner than usual. Lyric looked at her.

"*Don't* look at me," Tessa demanded.

"What's *your* problem?" Lyric replied.

"Her bracelet is missing," Savannah said.

I wondered where Bertha went. She used to be with them all the time. Maybe she was in another school. Why was I talking about *this?* I should have been talking about Anna being the culprit. I didn't know how she did it, but what she did was…*un*believable.

"You." Sunshine pointed at Anna, glancing at her bracelet. "You stole it."

"I didn't steal anything," Anna said defensively. Anna looked at her bracelet. "If you want your bracelet back, why don't you find it?"

Sunshine looked stunned. I was stunned too. Anna was usually shy and stuff. Not brave and confident.

"I did," Sunshine replied.

"Where?"

There was a bang. "Girls, sit down!" Ms. Wagner, the gym teacher, yelled. We all sat down immediately and I realized people were watching us. I leaned my back against the wall.

A colorful bracelet caught my eye. The bracelet was right next to me and so was that seventh grade girl.

"Hi," I said.

"Hi," she replied.

"Is that yours?"

"Actually, no. I found it on the locker room floor just a few moments ago. Do you want it?"

"Did you see that girl who snapped at my friend?"

"Yeah. I'm sure everyone did," she remarked.

"She's the one who needs it."

"Really," the girl said.

"Yes. It's hers. Who are you?" I finally asked. I know I should have asked her this before, but I wanted to know the important details first.

"Sadie Young," she replied.

"Sixth graders do laps," Ms. Wagner instructed as she sipped her coffee. Ms. Wagner was always drinking coffee. As a matter of fact, all my teachers drank coffee.

"I have her bracelet," I told Lyric.

"Give it to me. I'll give it to her," my friend replied.

"Okay. Here." I gave her the circular object and she looked at it as if it were gold. She jogged faster until she was standing next to Tessa. Tessa hugged her and said something. They talked until it was time to stop doing laps.

CHAPTER FOURTEEN

*O*h my goodness! What were they *talking about? She's mean and Lyric is nice. Tessa doesn't do anything for anyone. I should know!* I thought.

Lyric came back and acted normal. She didn't even tell me what she said. Something was going on and I wasn't going to find out what it was. I mean, I wanted to know what they were talking about, but that was a lot of work. She'd tell me when she was ready. As I was in Ms. Class' class, I looked behind me.

Jaxon wasn't even there. Maybe he was… I really didn't want to admit it because I didn't want to think of him as mean or I knew it was mean of him to beat his own friend up, but I still thought he was cute.

Ms. Class was looking at me. "Class, do page seventy-five in your workbook," she instructed. My teacher was walking toward me. "Come with me."

"Okay." Was I getting in trouble? I hoped not. She was staring at me again.

"Hello," I greeted her.

She waved at me. "I know you like Jaxon."

I could feel myself blush. "How do you know?" When it came out of my mouth, I knew I was a total giveaway.

"Don't you remember that day when you kissed him?" she replied. I couldn't believe she was talking to me about this.

"I didn't kiss him. Tessa did that." I felt myself get angry. "We tried to tell you and you believed Tessa. She's mean. And you…" My voice trailed off as tears trickled down my face and I ran away to the bathroom, which was right across from our classroom.

There were two girls there already. They were talking but I just ignored them until one of them said: "Do you know what his name is?"

"Jaxon. He is so cute!" another girl said. I stood up on the seat to take a sneak peek at who was talking. Nobody I knew. It was a girl who was putting on too much lip gloss and one who was looking inside of a purse.

"I know. And he could fight. That fight was *nice*," the one who was putting on too much gloss said.

I got down and flushed the toilet. I put a lot of soap on my hands.

"You're really going to waste *all* of that?" the girl who was digging in the purse remarked. She looked at me and I knew immediately who it was: Sadie Young. "Hello?"

"Hi, Sadie," I replied.

"You know this girl?" Too Much Lip Gloss questioned.

"Yeah…"

"You were talking to *her*?"

"What's the problem, Yaretzi?"

Yaretzi looked me up and down.

"She's U-G-L-Y," she whispered.

"I can spell, you know that, right? Unless…you're D-U-M-B!" I replied.

"Do you really want to mess with me?" Yaretzi asked. "I can beat you up any day."

Sadie jumped between us. "Um…I think you should leave," she advised.

CHAPTER FIFTEEN

I ran away. I ran away from the bathroom, soap still on my hands as I wiped them on my black pants. I went inside the classroom and everyone turned to stare at me. I was breathing heavily.

I took my seat and everyone was *still* looking at me.

"Um, Brylee?" Ms. Class said.

"Yeah. Brylee," Tessa said. She didn't say it in a mean way either. She said it in a *nice* way.

"Jaxon…" Tessa began.

"Not coming back for some time," Ms. Class informed me.

"Why?" I asked.

Tessa walked up to me and put a warm, manicured hand on my shoulder. "He was fighting with Reese. Reese isn't even here," Tessa answered. Tessa was being so nice to me. Why?

"Is he coming back?" I asked in a bored voice. The thing was that I didn't even care if Jaxon ever came back. I didn't even like him anymore. But how did everyone know that?

"Nope. His parents heard about it and took him out of the school," Tessa explained.

"But why did Ms. Class say 'some time'?" I replied.

"She didn't want to hurt your feelings. I'm sorry." She smiled at me. Everyone was hushed. "We all know you like him."

"Who said?" I quizzed. She didn't answer me. All she did was walk away.

Ms. Class checked her white watch. "The bell is going to ring in just five minutes," she said.

CHAPTER SIXTEEN

As I walked down the hall, I looked down at my shoes. I didn't want anyone asking me about the Jaxon thing. However, something else did happen.

"Hi," Sadie greeted. I waved. She was with Yaretzi again. "She just wanted to tell you something."

"I don't want to hear anything from her. She was about to fight me," I replied.

"So?" Yaretzi asked. "I was…"

"Just leave me alone." I walked past them. I didn't know why she was trying to talk to me when she was trying to start problems.

"Brylee!" a voice called. I spun around and saw Anna, Charlie, Lyric, Megan, and two other girls who looked exactly the same.

"Where are you going?" Anna asked me.

"French," I answered. I dreaded French class because all the teacher did was scream at us. On the bright side, I could finish my homework earlier.

"Why are you walking alone?" one of the twins asked.

"Um, who are you?" Then I remembered seeing both of them when Brynn was standing up for me.

"I am Ellie," the one with earrings introduced herself. She held a hand for me to shake. "Ellie Conway."

"Leslie Conway," the one without earrings said.

"I'm Brylee," I said as I shook both of their hands.

"C'mon," Anna urged. "Let's go to French." We all walked arms abreast. I finally had all the friends I needed.

"Do you hear a loud stomping noise?" Ellie questioned.

We all quieted down. "Yeah. What's that?" Lyric asked.

I turned around and sure enough Sadie and Yaretzi were following us. Yaretzi waved at me. I rolled my eyes.

"I need to talk to you," Yaretzi pleaded.

"You want to talk to me?" I said sarcastically.

"Seriously. I don't blame you for getting your attitude at me, but I'm S-O-R-R-Y," she apologized.

I laughed. I forgave her. "S-O-R-R-Y, too." We hugged as if we were two best friends.

"Hall sweep!" Assistant Principal Barr screamed.

"We better hurry up," Megan advised.

We all ran. I started laughing. Before all of this happened, I would have been running by myself. But now I wasn't. I was around people who were friendly to me.

"Bye," Yaretzi and Sadie said.

"Bye," I replied. I took my seat next to Megan.

"Who were they?" Megan asked.

"Two of my new friends." I smiled as I said that.

"Do you want to know something disturbing?" Megan questioned.

I shrugged. "Yeah."

"Jaxon and Sunshine are step brother and sister."

My jaw dropped. No wonder she was so mean to me and Lyric.

"I know. Gross."

I rolled my eyes.

"SHUT UP!" Ms. Vallee screamed. Megan and I giggled. "Stop laughing!"

Tessa, who sat across from us, glared at us as if she hated seeing me happy. Maybe she did. I didn't care. I was living my own life and I *loved* it.

Then a thought popped in my head.

"How did everyone know that I like Jaxon?" I quizzed.

Megan leaned in and said, "Tessa told everyone."

"Oh well." Tessa was still looking at me. "Hi, Tessa."

"Leave me alone," Tessa remarked. It was too good to be true. The only reason she was so nice to me was because she thought I was feeling upset about Jaxon. But now that she knew I was happy, *she was* angry.

CHAPTER SEVENTEEN

I sat in front of my computer screen, and the phone rang. My sister picked it up and talked on it for a while.

"It's your *crazy* friend," Brynn said. And I knew she was talking about Megan. At the dinner table she was always talking about Megan and how she was so crazy.

"Hey," I said.

"What?" Brynn replied.

"How's Azura?"

Brynn smiled. "She's doing fine. I'll tell you the story later."

"Hello?" I said into the phone.

"Hi. I just called you for the homework and to ask you if you can come to my house. My family members want to see the new baby my mom had last week."

"And you didn't even tell me!?"

We talked and talked about the baby, her family members, and the homework.

As I went to sleep, I thought about my new social life. It was great. Then I drifted off to sleep.

"Hello!" Sadie said as I came into the school yard. "You should have come here earlier."

"Why?" I asked.

"You made me study for my Spanish test!" Sadie exclaimed dramatically.

I rolled my eyes. "So?"

"I didn't *feel* like it."

I shook my head. "You're in the Drama Club, aren't you?"

"No. I'm in the Debate Club."

I was surprised. "How come?"

"There was no more room for me."

"FIGHT! FIGHT! FIGHT!" the crowd yelled. *Not again*, I thought.

"Who's fighting?" Megan asked, coming out of nowhere.

"OMG! This is so exciting!" Sadie screamed, grabbing both my and Megan's hands.

"Oh my goodness! It's Sunshine!" Megan said in a shocked voice.

"With Tessa." I couldn't even blink. I was so shocked. Why would they be fighting? Besides, this early in the morning?

Tessa slapped Sunshine in the face.

"Well, Sunshine is *not* filled with sunshine," Sadie observed. Sunshine was really angry. Tears were coming down her face. Tessa was laughing and enjoying it.

"Why is Tessa laughing?" Megan asked.

"I don't know," I said.

Then I heard a loud whistle. "Hey!" a boy screamed.

I laughed.

"What's so funny?"

"Oh, nothing."

"It better be!"

"I think that's Mr. Barr's son," Megan said.

"He is. He's in my class. He is so annoying! Every time someone talks while the teacher talks and the teacher gets mad he'll say, 'Hey!'" Sadie commented.

"HEY!" he screamed.

"What's his name?" Megan asked.

"Hey!" I answered.

We started to crack up. Everyone turned to see who was screaming. Even Tessa and Sunshine.

"Yeah! I said it. HEY!" Now everyone started to laugh.

"HEY! HEY! HEY!" everyone chanted.

"That's right! HEY!"

"Hey!" people screamed. Everyone started to laugh. Then all my friends came.

"We could hear people screaming from the other side of the school," Leslie said.

"Hey!" we cried. The three of us laughed, but not the rest of them. They didn't get it.

"What's so funny?" Anna quizzed.

"You..." I began but couldn't continue. It was just way too funny.

"What?" Lyric said.

"Nothing," Megan replied.

CHAPTER EIGHTEEN

It was a Saturday night. I was at Megan's house, looking over the crib. The baby was so cute. She was playing with her tiny baby feet.

"She is so cute!" I complimented.

"I know," Megan replied. "Do you want to see my cousin?"

"Your cousin?" Then the cutest boy walked into the room. Even cuter than Jaxon.

"I think I'm in love," I whispered to Megan.

"I think he's in love too."

"Hi," he said shyly.

"Hey," I replied.

"C'mon. Let's get acquainted." *He is such a gentleman*, I thought.

He held me by the hand. My new social life was the best one I'd ever had!

CHAPTER NINETEEN

"So he held your hand?" Leslie asked.

We were in Ellie and Leslie's bedroom. It was the day after Megan's baby shower.

"Did you get his number?" Ellie questioned.

"Yeah," I said.

"Call him!" Anna demanded.

I shook my head. "That is sort of private."

Lyric rolled her eyes. "How? We *are* your friends, aren't we?"

"Yeah. Although, this part of my life is supposed to be private."

"Yeah. Do you think Sunshine will be okay?" Charlie asked.

"I don't know," Ellie said.

"Forget her. Let's just enjoy our life. Agreed?"

"Agreed!" my friends roared.

"Do you want to play some card games?" Leslie asked.

"Okay," Charlie decided for us.

CPSIA information can be obtained at www.ICGtesting.com
Printed in the USA
BVOW081957270812

298952BV00001B/48/P